WAKE ME UP IN 20 COCONUTS!

Laurie Keller

I think r's are so comfy.

Hi, cute butterfly!

COCONUTS

Christy Ottaviano Books

LITTLE, BROWN AND COMPANY
New York   Boston

For my dear friend Jenny

A thank-you song to Christy Ottaviano,
to be sung to *Lady Marmalade* by (Patti) Labelle:

Thanks Otie, yay Otie, go Otie, love Otie
Thanks Otie, yay Otie, go Otie, love Otie
I met Otie O down in old NYC
Struttin' her pen on the street
She said, "Hello, LK—I think it's your lucky day!" (mm-hmm)
Thinky inky write it blah-blah
Scritchy scratchy change it here
Read it, edit, get it done now
Lovely Christy Otie-O
Voulez-vous publier un livre, avec moi?
Voulez-vous publier un livre?

ABOUT THIS BOOK

The illustrations for this book were done in acrylic, markers, watercolor, collage, and Photoshop. This book was edited by Christy Ottaviano and designed by Patrick Collins. The production was supervised by Nyamekye Waliyaya, and the production editor was Marisa Finkelstein. The text was set in LunchBox Slab, and the display type is hand lettered.

· Christy Ottaviano Books · Hachette Book Group · 1290 Avenue of the Americas, New York, NY 10104 · Visit us at LBYR.com · First Edition: September 2022 · Christy Ottaviano Books is an imprint of Little, Brown and Company. · The Christy Ottaviano Books name and logo are trademarks of Hachette Book Group, Inc. The publisher is not responsible for websites (or their content) that are not owned by the publisher. · Library of Congress Cataloging-in-Publication Data · Names: Keller, Laurie, author, illustrator. · Title: Wake me up in 20 coconuts! / Laurie Keller. Other titles: Wake me up in twenty coconuts! · Description: First edition. | New York : Little, Brown and Company, 2022. | "Christy Ottaviano Books." | Audience: Ages 4–8. | Summary: "Two quirky characters living in an apartment building come together in this picture book that reinforces the importance of asking questions in order to better understand each other and the world around them." —Provided by publisher · Identifiers: LCCN 2021051007 | ISBN 9780316311960 (hardcover) · Subjects: CYAC: Questions and answers—Fiction. | Neighbors—Fiction. | LCGFT: Picture books. · Classification: LCC PZ7.K281346 Wak 2022 | DDC [E]—dc23 LC record available at https://lccn.loc.gov/2021051007 · ISBN 978-0-316-31196-0 PRINTED IN CHINA · APS · 10 9 8 7 6 5 4 3 2 1

Acorn?

My alarm clock just broke. Would you wake me up in 20 coconuts, please?

Abso-COCONUT-ly, 2B!

I like being a helpful neighbor.
There's just one problem—
I don't know what
"WAKE ME UP IN 20 COCONUTS"
means!

I can't NOT KNOW something. I'm the KNOW-IT-ALL neighbor!

I come from a long line of KNOW-IT-ALLS, and "I DON'T KNOW" is something we just DON'T say.

Until TODAY, that is!

WAKE ME UP IN 20 COCONUTS.

That's the silliest thing I've ever heard! Did 2B make up some new way of telling time?

WAKE ME UP IN 20 COCONUTS.

Should I ask her what it means? I CAN'T ask her what it means. Then she'll know I don't know.

Okay, 2C, do the math.

How many COCONUTS in a MINUTE?

How many MINUTES in a COCONUT?

Oooh, what's THIS?

So 2B really DID ask me to wake her up in 20 coconuts. Why is she talking in coconut time?!

I'd better check.

All the wires are connected.

All the switches are on.

There's nothing rattling.

Maybe it just needs a cleaning.

Hey, Wally, can you squeeze me in today?

I bet I'll understand
COCONUT TIME
now that my brain is
shiny and clean!

Well...DO I?

WAKE ME
UP IN 20
COCONUTS!

NO! I don't get it!
What's WRONG with me?!

Sorry,
PHONEY.

PHONEY!
That's IT!

PHONEY will know what
"WAKE ME UP IN 20 COCONUTS"
smeans!

WHAT?! NOOOO!!!

Even PHONEY is talking in COCONUT TIME!

I CAN'T TAKE IT ANYMORE! COCONUT TIME IS DRIVING ME COCONUTTY!

Hey, 2C—nice hair and bucket! Anyway, thank you for waking me up in 20 coconuts!

20 coconuts exactly, 2C!

PHEW!

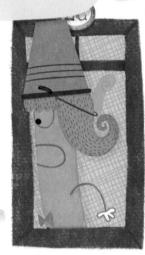

Would you wake me up in 20 coconuts tomorrow, too?

NO, 2B! I CAN'T WAKE YOU UP IN 20 COCONUTS EVER AGAIN!!!

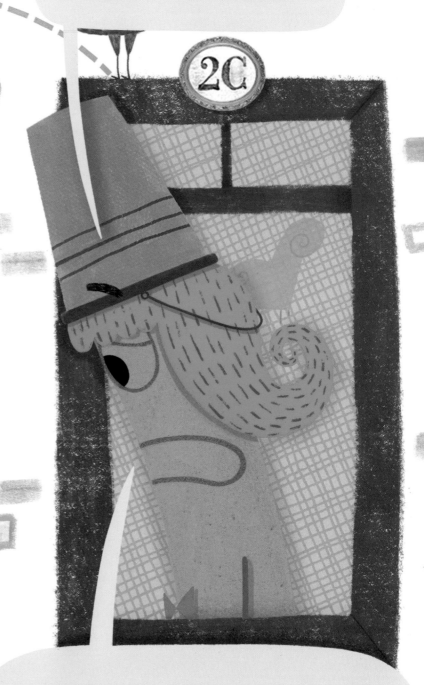

Why didn't you just tell me you don't know what "WAKE ME UP IN 20 COCONUTS" means, 2C?

I didn't want to look ridiculous.

A Note from Some Brains

We Brains just wanted to let you know that it's A-OK with us when you say "I DON'T KNOW"—in fact, we like it! That's because we get super excited to learn new things. We hope when people don't know something they'll go in search of answers because learning makes us grow bigger and stronger. Saying "I DON'T KNOW" is nothing to be embarrassed about. It actually shows how confident you are to admit you don't know something and that you have a curious brain that is eager to learn more. So next time you don't know something, make a point to get yourself some answers! Your brain will be even happier and smarter than it already is. And you'll give it something new to talk about at parties! WOO-HOO!

Thanks, everyone!
Your pals, the Brains